Some Surprise!

HANK JENKINS pressed his nose against the train window.

"Hey, fellers!" he cried. "We're coming into the station."

The train was bringing home the boys of Beaver Lake Camp. The summer was really over.

Hank had made sure that he would have only one thing to carry on the train. And he was taking mighty good care of that. It was a large metal cage and he held it firmly on his lap.

"You sure are lucky, Hank," said Marty Miller, who was sitting next to him. "Imagine bringing home a snake! You're lucky your mother doesn't mind."

"W — well," said Hank slowly, "she doesn't exactly know it's a snake. I just wrote that I had a surprise."

"Some surprise!" Marty grinned.

"Just wait till she sees how smart Puffy is," Hank said, a little more hopefully than he felt. He looked fondly at his snake. Puffy lay peacefully coiled in his cage — a yellow-speckled snake, two feet long, with dark brown bands on his body.

The train puffed and whined and slowed at last to a stop. Eagerly, Hank searched the faces of the crowd of people waiting to meet the campers.

The first person he spotted was his little brother Benjamin. There he was, hopping up and down as usual. And there was his sister Elizabeth! She had done something silly with her hair again. Where was his mother? Oh, yes. Right behind Liz!

Hank took another look at Puffy. Suddenly he put down the cage and pulled off his sweater.

"What are you doing, Hank?" asked Marty.

Hank dropped the sweater over the cage to cover it. "No sense rushing things," he replied.

Benjy was the first to greet Hank as he got off the train.

"Hank! Hank! Here I am!" Benjy cried. "Mommy says I can go to Beaver Lake Camp with you next summer if my allergies are okay. What've you got there?"

"Hi, Benjy." Hank put his arm around Benjy's shoulder for a minute. "Where's your front tooth?"

"It fell out yesterday," Benjy said proudly, "and I got a quarter for it!"

"A quarter!" cried Hank, shocked. "I never got more than a dime for a tooth of mine!"

Mrs. Jenkins and Liz came hurrying over.

"Hi, Mom!" Hank permitted his mother to give him a quick hug. Liz better not try any hugging, he thought fiercely.

But Liz just yelled, "Hello, Hank! You look ter*riff!*" Then she began talking a mile a minute to Dick Weller, who was fifteen years old. Hank shook his head. Dick was the best pitcher at

Beaver Lake Camp. It beat anything why he would stop to gab with a girl, especially Liz.

"Hank, dear, you look wonderful," said his mother, beaming at him. "Where's your bag? I found a place to park right down the street."

"I packed all my stuff in my trunk, Mom," Hank said quickly. "I just have this to carry."

Mrs. Jenkins did not even glance at the covered cage. She was eager to get to the car.

"Mom, can I ride home with the Wellers?" Liz called.

"All right," said Mrs. Jenkins. "But don't be home late. Come *on*, Benjy! This way, Hank."

Hank sat in the back of the car, Benjy in front with Mrs. Jenkins. All the way home, Hank kept the cage close beside him. He scarcely heard the questions his mother popped at him, or the bits of news she told him.

Benjy kept turning around and leaning over the back of his seat. "What've you got in the cage, Hank?" he asked.

"A surprise."

"For me?"

"No," Hank said firmly. "Not for you. He's my new pet."

"Can't I just take a peek?"

Hank shook his head. "Not till we get home."

"Aw, I bet it's just another old hamster," said Benjy.

"It is *not* a hamster," Hank said loudly. His mother had never really liked the cute little hamster he had last year.

"My, it's good to have you back, Hank," his mother said, smiling at him as they entered the house.

"Now let's see what's in the cage," cried Benjy, grabbing for the sweater.

"Cut it out, Benjy!" Hank said sharply. Then he bent down and pulled the sweater off the cage himself.

Benjy let out a joyous yell. "Oh, boy! A snake!"

"Isn't he a beauty, Mom?" asked Hank.

Mrs. Jenkins did not answer.

She just stood and stared.

Who Wants a Snake?

AFTER A moment Mrs. Jenkins found her voice.

"Hank," she asked, pointing to Puffy, "what in the world do you expect to do with — with — *that?*"

"He's my pet, Mom."

"That — that snake?"

"Puffy isn't just any old kind of snake," Hank said earnestly. "He's a hog-nosed snake."

His mother didn't look impressed, so Hank hurried to explain. "He's fun. He's harmless as anything. But he can look real fierce and scary. And look at this, Mom! Just watch!"

Hank leaned over and poked Puffy. Then he clapped his hands sharply. Puffy rolled over on his back and lay stiff and still.

Benjy watched, wide-eyed. "What's the matter with him, Hank?" he cried anxiously. "Is he dead?" Puffy did indeed look very dead.

Hank laughed. He opened the door of the cage and reached in. Gently he turned Puffy over. But Puffy rolled right over again on his back, looking as dead as ever.

"Isn't that wonderful, Mom?" Hank cried. "Did you see the way he plays dead?"

"Hank," said his mother, "did you expect to keep that snake *in this house*?"

"Sure, Mom. I'm very good with snakes. My counselor told me so. Father said so, too. He said Puffy was just great!"

"Just when did Father say all that?" asked Mrs. Jenkins.

"You know. When he stopped off at camp last Saturday. On his way to Chicago. He said Puffy was a fine — a fine — specimen — that's it!"

"And what did Father say about bringing him

home?" Mrs. Jenkins went on sternly.

"Well," said Hank slowly, "I didn't exactly ask him."

"Hank," said his mother, "you and I had better have a talk. Come over here and sit down."

Hank sat down unhappily beside his mother. Benjy trotted along and sat down beside Hank, eager not to miss a thing.

"I know you'd like to keep your snake, Hank," his mother said. "But I have to tell you how I feel about it. School starts next Monday. You're going to be a very busy boy. I'd be spending more time with your snake than you would. And believe me, Hank, *I* don't want a pet snake!"

"I could help," Benjy cried enthusiastically. "I could play dead with him!"

Hank turned angrily on his brother. "Don't you touch Puffy!" he cried.

"That's all I need," said Mrs. Jenkins, shaking her head. "You two scrapping over a snake! I'm sorry, Hank. I know you're unhappy about it. But you'll have to do something about that snake right away . . . well, anyway, before school starts. Maybe Mr. MacGregor at the pet shop would like to have him."

She gave Puffy a long, unfriendly look. Then she said firmly, "I know one thing — he can't live here!"

Hank walked slowly upstairs to his room. Deep in gloom, he set Puffy's cage down and looked around.

It was a room he had to share with his little brother. Nothing of his, thought Hank, was ever really safe from that kid.

Hank wandered around the room now, looking carefully at his models and collections. What damage had Benjy done while he was away at camp?

Everything seemed all right. But Hank couldn't even feel glad about that. He was much too unhappy about Puffy.

He walked back to the cage. Gently, he lifted Puffy out, all twenty-four speckled inches of him.

He held Puffy's head with its funny nose,

turned up like a hog's snout, and Puffy stretched out comfortably along Hank's arm. "Hello, Puff," Hank said softly. Boy, he was beautiful! The best pet he'd had all summer. Better than the turtle. Though it would have been fun to keep the turtle and see if it really lived for twenty-five years.

Get rid of Puffy! Hank sighed deeply.

He couldn't even ask his father to help explain things to his mother, as he sometimes did. Why, by the time his father got back from that business trip to Chicago, school would have been open for weeks.

Hank stroked Puffy's back. Maybe his mother had Puffy mixed up with a rattlesnake or something. Maybe he could get a book from the library — a book about snakes that she could read. . . .

No, it wouldn't do any good. He knew that. He'd better get his things unpacked. And he'd better get over to MacGregor's Pet Shop as fast as he could.

Mr. MacGregor was feeding some fish in a big glass tank when Hank walked in, carrying Puffy.

"Good afternoon, young man," said Mr. MacGregor cheerfully. "What can I do for you?"

Hank put Puffy's cage on the counter. All the way over he had been hoping hard that Mr. MacGregor liked snakes.

Mr. MacGregor peered into the cage.

"A hog-nosed snake, eh?" he said with great interest. He opened the cage and took out the snake. "He's a fine-looking fellow."

Hank was beginning to breathe a little easier.

"Yes, a very fine snake," Mr. MacGregor repeated. "By the way, do you know what these fellows are sometimes called?"

"Sure," said Hank proudly. "Puff adders! That's because they puff up and look so fierce when they're scared. They're supposed to look like real adders then, aren't they?"

"Right!" said Mr. MacGregor. "I've seen many of these puff adders in my day. But, of course," he added, "none quite so handsome as yours!"

Hank was feeling better every minute. "What do you think my snake is worth, Mr. Mac-Gregor?" he asked anxiously.

The man stood back and squinted at Puffy.

After a moment he said, "My boy, he's priceless!"

Hank was a bit confused by this wholly unexpected reply. Then he said eagerly, "You can have Puffy for nothing then, Mr. MacGregor."

Mr. MacGregor heaved a sigh. "My boy, that's a fine, generous offer. I wish I could accept it. But I once had a snake in here. You wouldn't believe what happened. Nobody wanted to come in. No, I'm sorry. I can't take him."

"People are awful funny about snakes, aren't they, Mr. MacGregor?" Hank said sadly.

"They are indeed," said Mr. MacGregor.

Now Hank had to figure out something else to do. Perhaps he should get in touch with a big circus. They'd surely want a snake as interesting as Puffy.

Carrying the cage, Hank walked slowly homeward. He was thinking so hard that he almost ran into Timmy Watts.

"Hi!" Timmy cried happily. "Where you going?"

"Nowhere," said Hank coldly. Timmy was not quite eight, and sometimes he was a real pest.

Timmy tried to keep up with Hank as they walked along. Suddenly, he yelled, "Hey, that's a snake!"

Hank did not bother to reply.

"Oh, boy, I wish I had a snake like that!" said Timmy admiringly.

Hank gave Timmy a very thoughtful look. If Puffy were in a circus, why, Hank would never see him. But Timmy lived only three blocks away.... All at once, Hank began to feel a lot more cheerful.

"It's not easy to find a snake like this," he told Timmy. He stopped and put down the cage. "Just watch this!"

Hank rolled up his sleeves. He began to wave his hands around the cage in a mysterious way. Then in a deep voice he said, "Hocus! Pocus! Willa — walla — woo!"

He gave Puffy a hard poke and put him through his trick of playing dead.

"Say, that's neat!" cried Timmy.

"Would you like to hold him for a minute?" Hank asked in a kindly voice.

"Can I really?" Timmy's eyes almost popped out of his head.

"Of course, I wouldn't let just *anybody* hold him," Hank explained as he lifted Puffy out of the cage.

He showed Timmy how to hold Puffy's head and let the snake coil around his arm.

Timmy was still breathless as Hank put Puffy back.

"You know," said Hank, "a person with an unusual snake like this. . . . Well, there are lots of things a person could do when he grows up. For instance — "

"For instance?" asked Timmy.

"Well, a person with an unusual snake like this could be . . . well, a snake charmer, for instance."

"You mean, like in a circus?"

Hank nodded wisely. "And you know what else? A person with a snake like this could even join the — The Royal Order of Snake Charmers!"

"No kidding?" said Timmy. Then he added, "What's that?"

Hank looked scornful. "It's only the most important Order of Snake Charmers in the world, that's all!"

Timmy was quiet for a moment. "Where do you get snakes like that?" he asked.

"Oh, they're hard to get, I admit. Of course, *I* could always get another one, but for you, it's pretty hopeless. Unless. . . ." He stopped as if an idea had suddenly struck him.

"Unless what?" Timmy asked.

"Unless I let you have Puffy," Hank said, watching Timmy's face.

"Would you, Hank? Would you really?"

Hank looked very serious. Then he clapped Timmy on the back and said heartily, "All right, Timmy, I'll let you have my snake!"

Timmy could hardly catch his breath. "Oh, boy! Thanks, Hank! Thanks a lot!"

"I'll lend you the cage, too," said Hank generously. "Till you can get another one. Better get him home now, Timmy, in time for his afternoon nap."

Still looking a little dazed, Timmy took off with his new snake.

Hank was very pleased with himself. He whistled all the way home.

Twenty minutes after he got home his doorbell rang. There on the doorstep was Timmy Watts, with Puffy.

"Here, Hank," said Timmy, holding up the cage.

"What's the matter?" asked Hank. "Don't you care about the Royal Order — "

"My mother said NO."

"Didn't you explain about — "

"She said ABSOLUTELY NO. She said lots more, too. She said you — "

"Never mind," said Hank quickly, and he took back the cage.

"Oh, Puffy," Hank whispered to his snake, "I'm really glad you're back." But he wondered what his mother was going to say. School began on Monday — and Puffy was still around.

More Worries

To HANK'S surprise, his mother did not say anything more about Puffy.

Not that day or the next.

Hank could see that it was only because she was so busy getting school clothes ready, but he was glad anyway.

The more time he had to figure out what to do about Puffy, the better. He decided that meanwhile it might be a good idea if both he and Puffy stayed out of his mother's way as much as possible.

He even tried helping to Keep Her Mind Off Unpleasant Things. Saturday morning, for instance, he said very brightly, "Want me to help set the table, Mom?"

He could see that his mother was pleased. So at lunchtime he asked very sweetly, "Want me to help dry the dishes, Mom?"

Mrs. Jenkins looked a little startled, but she only said, "Why, yes, dear. Thank you."

Later in the day he said, "Need anything at the store, Mom?"

Mrs. Jenkins put down some name tapes she was sewing on Benjy's clothes and came over to Hank. She put her hand on his forehead. "Do you feel all right, dear?" she asked, looking worried.

"Oh, sure, Mom," Hank said quickly. "I feel fine."

But he could see it would be best to go a bit slowly. Best not to overdo this business of helping his mother Forget Unpleasant Things.

It was really of no use, though. He still had the problem of what to do with Puffy. And school was only two days away! No one was helping Hank forget *that.*

Wherever he went, the house was full of a back-to-school-on-Monday bustle.

There was Liz trying to decide which of her

two new skirts to wear to school. Every time Hank looked at her, she had on a different one — first the red skirt, then the blue skirt, then the red one again.

Then her best friend, Janey Baker, had to see them on her — first the blue one, then the red one, then the blue one again!

Feeling very gloomy, Hank tried to escape to his room.

There was Benjy. For once, he wasn't suspiciously close to Puffy's cage.

Benjy was full of school-on-Monday, too! Benjy was going into the first grade and he was pretty excited about it.

There he was, marching around the room, carrying an old schoolbag of Hank's.

Hank watched him for a minute. "What do you think you're doing, anyway?" Hank asked. "You're not going into the U.S. Army, you know. You're only going into the first grade."

"They do so march in the first grade," said Benjy, parading around proudly with his bag.

That bag seemed just a little too full to Hank. "Say, what have you got in that bag?" he wanted to know.

"Things," said Benjy, with a wide-eyed look that Hank knew very well.

"Let's see what things." Hank grabbed the bag and opened it.

Just as he thought! Out came Hank's comic books. Out came his pencils. There were all his baseball cards.

Oh, no! Even his new airplane model — his F86 jet. And the right wing was split! "Look what you did to my model!" Hank cried hotly. "Look at that wing!"

"It's no good, anyway," said Benjy. "It's hard to fly."

"Listen, brat!" Hank told him angrily. "I'm the only one who's supposed to fly that!"

"And you're not supposed to call me 'brat,' " Benjy reminded him, looking very hurt.

Hank was just about to stalk out of the room and ask his mother please, PLEASE to make Benjy leave his things alone. Then he remembered that Puffy and he were staying out of her way.

It was bad enough to worry about going back to school with Puffy on his mind. Liz made it worse. At supper, she began talking again about Miss Tucker.

Miss Tucker taught the fourth grade. She was Hank's new teacher.

"Poor you," Liz said to Hank, "just wait till you find out what Miss Tucker is like. Is she strict!"

Hank pretended not to hear.

"Dearie me," he said in a squeaky voice, "should I wear my red pants or my sky-blue pants to school?"

"Fresh!" said Liz angrily. "But you just wait and see. Miss Tucker happens to be 'specially strict about spelling!"

"Dear me," Hank went on, more loudly. "I think I'll wear my pants with the purple polka dots. . . ."

"Hank!" said Mrs. Jenkins, sharply. "That will do."

"Poor Hank," Liz said again in her most sixth-grade voice. "I bet you have to stay in after school every day, learning how to spell *cat*."

"Liz," said Mrs. Jenkins, "stop teasing Hank."

Hank wondered. Was Liz just teasing?

Some of the kids did say Miss Tucker was strict.

Was she really strict about spelling? Or was Liz just saying that because she knew Hank wasn't a very good speller?

Boy, he had *some* worries.

What was he going to do about Puffy?

Suppose Miss Tucker did make kids stay in for spelling?

Hank gave a deep sigh.

The Fourth Grade
Gets a Job

"SAY, HANK," Marty Miller asked as they waited for the green light at the corner, "what did you do about Puffy?"

"Nothing," Hank said gloomily. "Nothing yet, I mean."

It was Monday morning, and they were both walking to school. Marty was in the fourth grade, too.

Hank was glad Marty had called for him. Especially on this first day of school.

"Hey, look at those peanuts in the third grade!" Marty said as they walked into the big school yard.

Hank suddenly felt quite tall as he looked over at the third-grade line.

"There's Stuey Wilson!" Marty cried. "And Freddie! And Sam!"

"Hi, Stu! Hi, Freddie!" Hank yelled. "Hey, Sam, here we are!" He greeted them happily like long-lost friends. It didn't matter that he had seen them only the day before.

Everybody on the fourth-grade line seemed to be talking at once. "I bet we get to run the school Post Office," said Marty. "That's what the fourth grade did last year."

"Post Office!" said Stuey Wilson scornfully. "I'd rather have charge of the milk and cookies!"

"Milk and cookies!" Betsy Baker tossed her head. "The fourth grade always gets an *important* job."

Betsy was Janey Baker's sister, and Hank always had fun teasing her. Except that he didn't feel much like teasing anyone right now.

Just then the bell rang. The lines in the yard started to move as the children began marching to their rooms.

The fourth grade was in Room Six.

"Good morning," said Miss Tucker pleasantly.

Hank stole a look at her. She was smiling. But that didn't mean anything, thought Hank. Not with a teacher.

Miss Tucker told the class where their seats were. Then she began to give out the books.

Hank reached for his first book with some excitement. He took one look at it. Then he dropped it as if it had taken a bite out of his hand.

The first book was a speller!

When all the books had been given out, Miss Tucker sat down at her desk and began to talk about what she had done during her vacation.

"I was on a real ranch this summer," she told the class. "I saw cowboys at work, and I learned to ride a horse." She laughed. "Not a bucking bronco, you may be sure. I was just a dude. I'd like to know what all of you did this summer."

Hank closed his eyes and tried to think of Miss Tucker on a real horse. He shook his head. A *teacher* on a horse! He couldn't imagine it.

He heard some of the other children telling

about their vacations. But he didn't really listen. Hank was thinking about Beaver Lake Camp, and the day he got Puffy. . . .

The teacher's voice broke in on Hank's thoughts. "Mrs. West, our principal, wants us to do a very special job this year," Miss Tucker was saying. "She wants us to take full charge of the Science Room. That means we would take care of it for the whole school."

Buddy Fisher waved his hand in the air. "I have some swell rocks I could bring," he said.

"Good!" said Miss Tucker. "We could start a rock collection."

Hands began to go up all over the room.

"I've got some seashells I found this summer."

"I've got a magnet. . . ."

Suddenly Hank's hand shot up, too, almost by itself. Then Hank heard himself saying in a loud voice, "Miss Tucker, I've got a pet snake."

He waited.

"Really?" said Miss Tucker.

"He's a beautiful snake," Hank went on breathlessly. "He's very, *very* harmless, Miss Tucker. He just looks fierce sometimes because he hisses

and puffs up, and his name is Puffy. . . ."

"Oh," said Miss Tucker, nodding her head. "You have a hog-nosed snake. They're very interesting snakes, aren't they?"

Hank could hardly believe it — Miss Tucker knew about hog-nosed snakes!

"Can I bring him, Miss Tucker? Can I bring him for the Science Room?"

"Well," said Miss Tucker, slowly, "keeping a snake in school wouldn't be easy."

"I have a good cage," Hank went on eagerly. "My counselor at camp helped me make it. It's got a sliding glass front and — and — everything. . . ."

"What about cleaning up after him?" Miss Tucker asked.

"I put newspapers in the cage," Hank said quickly. "That makes it easy to clean up."

Everyone in the class was listening now.

"Then there's the problem of feeding him," said Miss Tucker. "Hog-nosed snakes eat toads, don't they?"

"Oh!" The gasp came from Betsy.

"Shhhhh!" The shushing came from Marty.

"Puffy eats meat now," Hank said proudly. "I trained him this summer. I put a strip of meat on a stick and wiggle it. And he takes it every time."

"Would you be willing to take charge of your snake?" asked Miss Tucker.

"Oh, yes!" Hank drew in his breath. "Oh, yes, I would!"

Miss Tucker smiled. "Well, then," she said, "I don't see why we can't invite Puffy to our Science Room. Or at least give him a try."

Slowly, Hank sank into his seat. Liz must be crazy. Miss Tucker was super. Miss Tucker was the best teacher he ever had in his whole life.

Puffy Goes to School

"LOOK, STUEY, just look at him!" said Hank proudly.

Hank and Stuey Wilson were alone in the Science Room with Puffy.

It was Puffy's first morning at school.

Miss Tucker had said that Hank could spend part of the science period getting Puffy settled in his new home.

Yes, Stuey Wilson could help. "If you don't waste any time!" said Miss Tucker, giving them a long look.

"Oh, no!" said Hank, happily.

"Of course not!" said Stuey firmly. "You know us."

"Yes," said Miss Tucker. "That's what I mean!"

Now Hank was busy taking care of Puffy. "Look, Stuey," said Hank. "Isn't he a beauty?"

Stuey leaned on his elbows and watched Puffy resting lazily in his cage. "S'posing he was a cobra or something like that," said Stuey. His face lit up. "Say, wouldn't that be exciting?"

"I'd rather have him the way he is," said Hank, pouring some water into Puffy's dish.

"What's that you're giving him?" Stuey wanted to know.

"Water, of course," said Hank. "What did you think a snake drinks, ginger ale?"

Stuey thought about that. "What would happen if you gave him ginger ale?" he asked. "Would he burp?"

Hank was getting ready to put some stones in Puffy's cage. "You're supposed to be helping me," he reminded Stuey. "Watch the way this cage opens. It's tricky. Now you open it while I put these stones in."

Both boys were so busy with Puffy that they did not hear the door open. Neither of them saw Mrs. West, the principal, come into the room.

Mrs. West walked quietly over to see what

the two boys were finding so interesting. Looking over their heads, she saw Puffy.

"Eeeeeeeek!" Mrs. West didn't mean to, but she gave a little scream.

Hank was so startled he dropped the stone he was holding.

Stuey's elbows slipped off the table, and he almost toppled off his chair.

All this was too much for Puffy. He raised his head. He flattened out. Then he began to puff up. *"Hssssssssss!"* came from Puffy fiercely. *"Hsss!"*

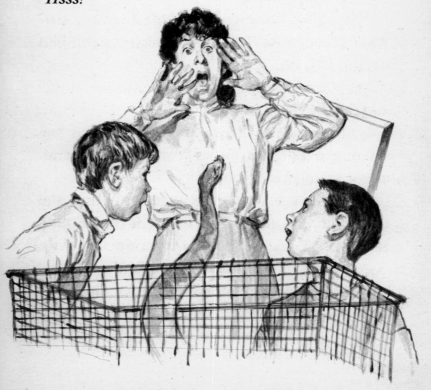

For a moment, Mrs. West seemed unable to speak. Then sternly she asked, "What is that snake doing here?"

"That's Puffy Jenkins," Stuey said helpfully. "He lives here."

At that moment, Miss Tucker walked in. "What in the world is going on — " she began crossly.

Then she saw the principal. "Mrs. West," said Miss Tucker, "I gave these boys permission to work in here."

Mrs. West pointed to Puffy.

"It's just a harmless hog-nosed snake, Mrs. West," said Miss Tucker. "Hank brought him for our Science Room."

"You're quite sure it's all right, Miss Tucker?" asked Mrs. West.

"Oh, yes," Miss Tucker replied. "Hank's had the snake as a pet all summer. He knows all about taking care of him."

Mrs. West walked to the door. Then she turned around and looked back. "If you're quite sure, Miss Tucker," she said from the doorway, "quite sure...." Quickly, she walked out.

Hank was worried. He could see that Mrs.

West wasn't quite sure at all about having Puffy in her school.

The very next day something happened at recess that made Hank worry even more.

The fourth grade was in the outside yard.

The boys were having relay races. Hank loved races. He was a good runner and his team won twice.

On the other side of the yard, the girls were jumping rope. Hank could hear that jump-rope song they were always singing.

Teddy Bear, Teddy Bear, turn around.
Teddy Bear, Teddy Bear, touch the ground.
Teddy Bear, Teddy Bear, show your shoe.
Teddy Bear, Teddy Bear, please skiddoo!

When the boys finished the second race, Miss Tucker looked at her watch. "We have about ten minutes left for a game of dodge ball," she told the boys. "Hank and Freddy, will you please get the ball? It's in the big closet in the back of the room."

Hank and Freddy raced off to get the ball.

As the two boys passed the girls, Jenny Brooks saw Hank. Jenny was one of the "enders." Suddenly she began to sing out,

Puffy Jenkins, Puffy Jenkins, turn around.
Puffy Jenkins, Puffy Jenkins, touch the ground.
Puffy Jenkins, Puffy Jenkins, show your shoe.
Puffy Jenkins, Puffy Jenkins, please skiddoo!

All the girls laughed. Even Hank thought it was funny to have Puffy in a jump-rope song. But then Hank heard Betsy say in a loud voice, "And that's what that awful snake should do, please SKIDDOO right away!"

Hank stopped short. "What's awful about my snake?" he wanted to know.

"He's horrible-looking!" Betsy retorted. "And my mother says it's disgusting to allow a snake in school, and he ought to be taken out right away!"

"Well," said Hank hotly, "that just shows how much your mother knows about snakes. . . ."

"Is that so!" said Betsy angrily. "Well, she knows they don't belong in school, which is more than some people standing right here know. And what's more, Smarty, she's going to speak to Mrs. West about it!"

Freddy was tugging at Hank's sleeve. "Aw, come on, Hank," he said. "We only have a few minutes left to play."

Hank went on with Freddy to get the ball. Of course Betsy was only fooling. Her mother wouldn't really speak to Mrs. West about Puffy.

Or would she?

A Snake Is Not a Snack

FOR THE first time in his life, Hank wanted to do his homework. His science homework, anyway.

His job was to make a sign for Puffy's cage. Miss Tucker called *that* homework. Hank had to laugh. Then he remembered his spelling paper. Four words wrong again.

Hank stopped on the way home from school to buy some black ink, a thick pen point, and some cardboard for the sign.

As he ran into the house, he heard Liz talking on the telephone. Hank grinned. It might be fun to pester his sister at the phone.

Then he heard his name. Liz was talking about him.

"Why, Hank is a real scientist," Liz was saying. She sounded angry. "I'm quite surprised at you, Janey Baker. That's a very ignorant way to talk."

Janey must have said something then to make Liz even angrier.

"That's the silliest thing I ever heard!" she retorted. "Betsy's just lucky there's someone in her class who knows as much as Hank does. Well, I don't care, either, if you don't come over. Good-bye!"

Hank was too astonished to move. Why, Liz was having a fight with her best friend about *him*. The fight must have been about Puffy. But Liz — Liz had a fight with Janey and she was sticking up for *him!* Why, he didn't know she thought he was a scientist.

Hank went quietly to his room. Suddenly he felt very glad he hadn't teased Liz at the telephone.

Right after supper, Hank sat down at the big dining-room table to make the sign for Puffy's cage. Benjy sat right down beside him.

"What're you going to do, Hank?" Benjy asked eagerly.

"I have to make a sign for Puffy's cage in the Science Room," Hank said in a you-can't-possibly-understand-this tone of voice.

"What kind of sign?" Benjy wanted to know.

"The kids in my class want it to say: PUFFY JENKINS, SNAKE," Hank replied. "Then I'm supposed to make up a talk about Puffy for all the other kids who come to see him."

Benjy jumped up and down. "Puffy Jenkins! He's my brother!"

Hank grabbed the cardboard which Benjy almost knocked off the table.

"Why don't you scram — disappear — vamoose?" he cried.

Benjy sat down quietly. "Can't I watch you?" he begged. "I won't do anything. Honest."

"Go watch TV," Hank told him. "Go ride your bike. Go away!"

"Please. . . ."

Benjy looked so disappointed that Hank sighed and said, "Okay, okay. But don't bother me!"

First Hank printed his sign in pencil. When

he liked the way it looked, he began to go over the words in ink. He worked slowly and carefully.

Watching every move of Hank's hand, Benjy came closer and closer.

Suddenly it happened.

Benjy's elbow tipped the bottle of ink. A thick black stream spilled slowly across Hank's sign.

Hank jumped to his feet with a yell. "Look what you did!" he screamed. "Look what you did!"

Benjy was frightened. He moved quickly to the other side of the table, near the door.

Liz ran into the room. "What happened?" she cried.

Hank could hardly speak. He pointed to the sign. "Look what he did!"

Liz looked at the sign. "Hank," she said gently, "that sign wasn't any good, anyway. You spelled *snake* wrong. You wrote PUFFY JENKINS, SNACK."

Hank stared at the sign in horror. Suppose he had brought that sign in! He could just hear all the kids laughing. . . .

He sat down weakly. Liz sat down beside him. "Look, Hank!" She picked up his pencil and wrote on the cardboard. "Snake. S-N-A-K-E. The *E* at the end makes it say *snake*. The *E* makes the *A* say its name. Get it?"

"S-n-a-k-e," Hank said slowly.

"Now spell *cake!*" said Liz quickly.

"Like *snake?*" Hank asked.

Liz nodded.

"C-a-k-e?" Hank tried it.

"Right!" said Liz. "Now spell *take.*"

"T-a-k-e," Hank said quickly. He laughed. "And

lake — l-a-k-e. *Fake* — f-a-k-e. Right?"

Liz stood up. "Right! I'll help you with your spelling homework if you want me to. I know a lot of spelling tricks."

"Okay," said Hank. "Right after I m-a-k-e this sign!"

Benjy had been standing behind the door, listening. He was not quite sure which way he would have to go. He was prepared to move fast. Now he stuck his head in the doorway.

"See! Aren't you glad I made you do it over?"

Hank took a step toward Benjy. But Benjy scooted out like a rabbit.

Then Hank sat down again to work. He made a beautiful sign. Clear as anything, it said: PUFFY JENKINS, SNAKE.

He put it carefully at the foot of his bed. It was the last thing he saw before he went to sleep.

And it was the first thing he saw the next morning.

Puffy Disappears

"SO YOU see, a hog-nosed snake like Puffy is really harmless and all that hissing and puffing I told you about is just so's no one will hurt him."

Hank finished in a rush of words. Then he took a deep breath. He had just made his speech about Puffy again. This time to the fifth grade.

He wasn't so nervous about doing it anymore. Not like the first time when he spoke to the second grade. Or even the next time to the third grade.

As the fifth grade walked out of the Science Room, Shorty Price whispered, "Say, that snake of yours is really super!" Hank beamed. After all, Shorty was the captain of the school baseball team.

Puffy had been in school for two weeks now. And the Science Room was "Open for Business," as Stuey put it.

The fourth grade was quite proud of the job it had done.

There was a rock collection and some sea-shells, neatly labeled, on one table. A strong magnet and a box of nails lay on another table. There were plants all around the room, too, and a good-sized fish tank with lots of guppies.

Freddie had sent away for a big Star Chart that one could get for box tops.

And the class was reading about raising hamsters.

But even now, the Science Room looked pretty good to the fourth grade.

And it was Puffy who made the biggest hit. Whenever a class came in, everybody crowded around his cage. They watched with delight when Hank took him out and held him. They listened eagerly to everything he told them about Puffy and hog-nosed snakes.

Yes, sir, thought Hank, Puffy was the best

thing in the whole Science Room — even though Betsy and some of her friends still pretended that he was "horrible."

Hank looked happily at his pet. "But we don't care what those dopey girls think, do we, Puff?"

Hank had one more talk to make this morning. And that was to the first grade. I hope Benjy isn't a pest, he thought anxiously. I hope he doesn't show off.

At ten o'clock Hank was back in the Science Room, ready for the first grade children. Miss Hill marched them in quietly.

Hank tried not to look at Benjy. But out of the corner of his eye he could see his little brother waving wildly to him. Hank pretended not to notice.

The children crowded wide-eyed around Puffy's cage. Benjy began jumping up and down. "That's Puffy Jenkins in that cage," he said in a loud whisper. "He's my brother!"

The children giggled. But Hank thought, that corny joke of his, and wouldn't even smile back.

Hank opened the cage and took Puffy out. Some of the children moved back quickly.

"Ooh! He's scary!" said a little girl.

"He won't hurt you," Hank said. He let some of the children touch Puffy. Then he told them all about his snake.

He hurried a little this time, because he was afraid that Benjy would spoil his talk.

But Benjy suddenly became very quiet.

Hank finished his speech and put Puffy back. Carefully, he closed the cage.

Miss Hill said she would take the children around the Science Room now and explain the other exhibits.

Hank was glad his talk to Benjy's class was over. Oh, I suppose I should have said hello to him or something, he thought for a moment.

Then he forgot about Benjy and ran back to the fourth grade room.

When he got back, his class was just beginning to write some letters. The fourth grade was inviting parents to come to school to see the Science Room.

"Hey, Hank," Stuey whispered, "you ought to get a letter, too!"

"Me?" Hank whispered back, puzzled.

"Sure," said Stuey. "You're a parent. You have Puffy Jenkins in school!" Stuey laughed so hard at his own joke that Miss Tucker looked at both of them with a frown.

Hank wrote his letter carefully. Maybe he

wouldn't have to do it over this time. He spelled *please* without looking in his spelling book. He stopped for a minute when he came to the word *visit.* Then he remembered the trick Liz showed him. "Say to yourself, 'Is it a visit?' " she had told him. *"Is it a visit?* Catch on?" And he got it right.

It was almost time for lunch when the letters were finished.

Just before the bell rang, Hank went back into the Science Room. It was his turn to see that the window was closed during lunch.

It was much too sunny in the Science Room, so Hank pulled the shade down, too. On his way out, he ran over to Puffy's cage to say, "So long, Puff. See you later."

Hank stopped at the cage and stared. Where was Puffy?

Quickly, he opened the door and moved the stones. He lifted the newspapers.

WHERE WAS PUFFY?

It took Hank about a full minute to believe it. Puffy was gone.

Who Did It?

No, IT couldn't be true.

Hank got down on his hands and knees. He began looking under the chairs and tables. "Puffy! Hey, Puffy?" he kept calling in a loud whisper.

Suppose Puffy got out into the street. He might be run over! Suppose he got scared and began to puff and hiss. People might think he was dangerous. They might even kill him!

A bell rang loudly.

Oh, no! Lunch! He had to get home for lunch! Hank gave a last desperate look around — behind the steam pipes, on the window sills, in every plant.

But there wasn't a sign of Puffy.

"I'll come back early," Hank said to himself as he started home for lunch. "I'll get back real early and find him."

All the way home, his head buzzed with questions. Where could Puffy be?

How did Puffy get out of his cage anyway?

"I locked that cage. I know I did!" he told himself again and again.

Well, then, how did Puffy get out?

By the time Hank got home, Liz had finished

her lunch. Benjy still sat at the table, chewing dreamily on his sandwich.

"You're awfully late, Hank," his mother scolded. "You'll just about have time to eat and get back."

"I don't want any lunch, Mom. I'm not hungry."

Mrs. Jenkins looked at Hank in astonishment. Most of the time she couldn't serve his lunch fast enough. "What's the matter?" she asked. "Is something wrong?"

Now, how did she know? Hank wondered. He wasn't going to tell anyone that Puffy was missing. Not until he had another chance to hunt for him.

But he was so full of worry that he blurted it out. "Puffy's gone, Mom!"

Benjy looked horrified. "How could Puffy be gone?"

"I can't figure it out," Hank said unhappily. "He got out of his cage somehow."

"Oh, dear!" cried his mother. "Imagine that snake loose in the school! Will you get into trouble, Hank?"

Benjy pushed his sandwich to one side. "I don't want any more," he told his mother.

Hank jumped up.

"I have to hurry, Mom. I have to get back to school early and look for Puffy."

"Can't you wait a few minutes and go back with Benjy?"

Benjy put his head down on the table. "I don't feel good, Mommy," he said. "I don't want to go back."

Mrs. Jenkins put her hand on Benjy's forehead. She frowned. "His head is a little warm. All right, Hank, run along. I just hope Benjy's allergy isn't acting up again."

On the way back to school Hank did some fast thinking. He had to find Puffy right away. Then he wouldn't even have to tell Miss Tucker — or anybody — that he had escaped.

Hank ran almost all the way back to school.

He dashed into the Science Room and over to Puffy's cage. "Please be back, Puffy," he said to himself. "Please be back in your cage when I look."

But he wasn't.

The bell clanged loudly, and Hank had to return to his classroom.

Miss Tucker gave out some papers, but Hank didn't even hear what she said was to be done with them.

He just sat and thought. How did Puffy get out of his cage? Where could he be now?

"Get to work, Hank," said Miss Tucker.

Hank raised his hand quickly. "May I get a drink, please?" he asked.

Miss Tucker nodded.

As soon as he was out in the hall, Hank started his frantic search for Puffy.

He began right outside the Science Room. He searched every step of the nearest stairway.

He stayed out as long as he dared. Then he hurried back to his room.

Miss Tucker was talking. But Hank was thinking. Puffy moved fast. He could be down in the basement by now. That's where Mr. O'Toole's office was.

Mr. O'Toole took care of the school building. He knew where everything was. Maybe he had seen Puffy.

I could sort of ask him, thought Hank.

As soon as he thought it would be all right, Hank asked to leave the room again.

Miss Tucker frowned, but she nodded anyway.

Hank almost flew downstairs to the basement.

Mr. O'Toole's door was open. Hank walked slowly by, trying to look as if he just happened to be strolling past.

His heart skipped a beat. Mr. O'Toole was in. "Hi, Mr. O'Toole," Hank said in a loud, cheerful voice.

"Hello, there, Hank. And did you come down here looking for some grasshoppers for your zoo?" Mr. O'Toole's eyes twinkled.

Hank made himself laugh. "I bet if there *were* any old grasshoppers around in this school you'd see them, wouldn't you, Mr. O'Toole?"

"Sure, Hank. I'm a regular big game hunter!" Mr. O'Toole laughed.

"I guess you do see lots of funny things down here sometimes, don't you?" Hank asked again.

"Oh, yes. Every day! All kinds of boys and girls."

"No. I mean, well, sometimes you might see a grasshopper — or — or — a snake or something like that?"

"Well, if I do, Hank," Mr. O'Toole nodded, "I'll bring it right up to the fourth grade zoo. By the way, how's that snake of yours?"

"Fine." Hank sighed. No, Mr. O'Toole hadn't seen Puffy, either.

Hank went sadly back to his room. As he came in, Miss Tucker was writing something on the blackboard.

She turned around and said quietly, "Please stay after the bell rings, Hank."

"Yes, Miss Tucker," and Hank slid into his seat meekly.

How did Puffy get out of that cage? Nobody else ever opened it, except Stuey.

Stuey....

Hank looked across the room at Stuey Wilson. Stuey was busy writing.

Would that be Stuey's idea of a joke, letting Puffy out?

Once Stuey looked up at Hank. But he didn't wink or make faces. He just looked away and went on writing.

"I bet it *was* Stuey," Hank said to himself. "He didn't even look me in the eye. He feels guilty. I bet it was Stuey!"

At three o'clock, Hank remembered that Miss Tucker wanted to see him.

He stood at the door and waited. "Sit down, Hank," said Miss Tucker. Then she added, "What's the matter, Hank? What's wrong?"

Hank gave a deep sigh. "Puffy's gone!"

"Oh, no!" Miss Tucker walked quickly into the Science Room with Hank at her heels.

She looked at the empty cage. "How did it happen? How did he get out?"

"I don't know, Miss Tucker. I locked the cage right after I had him out for the first grade kids. Honest, I did! Ask Miss Hill."

He watched Miss Tucker's face.

"We know Puffy couldn't get out unless the door was opened, don't we?" Miss Tucker said slowly. She seemed to be sad about something.

She thinks I forgot to close the door, Hank thought. He could tell her about Stuey! No, he couldn't. Even if he were sure, he couldn't tell a teacher something like that.

"What'll we do, Miss Tucker?"

"We can't do much right now," she replied. "We'll ask Mr. O'Toole to keep an eye open for Puffy till morning."

A terrible thought struck Hank. "Miss Tucker," he said in a small voice, "do we have to tell Mrs. West?"

Miss Tucker looked as if she didn't much like the idea herself. But all she said was, "Yes, Hank, I'm afraid we do."

The Great Snake Hunt

"THIS IS going to be some awful day!" That was the thought Hank woke up with next morning.

The day certainly started out that way.

Benjy still didn't feel well, and Mrs. Jenkins was worried.

Dr. Newman had come to see Benjy. But he was puzzled. "I can't find anything wrong," he told Mrs. Jenkins. "It doesn't look as though his allergy is to blame. Keep him in bed for another day, and let me know if there's any change."

Benjy just kept saying, "I don't feel good." He looked so pale and unhappy that Hank felt sorry for him.

On the way to school, Hank was busy feeling sorry for himself. He had figured out six different ways of telling Mrs. West about Puffy. But none of them sounded just right.

Then suddenly the day began to look more hopeful.

When he got to school, Hank learned that Mrs. West wasn't even in the building. She was away at a meeting. And, what was more, she'd be gone all day!

The sigh of relief that Hank gave seemed to come from his very toes.

Something else made him feel good, too.

That happened when Miss Tucker told the fourth grade about Puffy.

Everybody was excited. Everybody wanted to find Puffy.

"We ought to send out some searching parties, Miss Tucker!" That was Buddy Fisher's idea.

"We can't stop everything and look for Puffy," Miss Tucker said sharply. "We'll set up some committees. A few of you can take turns going out."

"Miss Tucker! Miss Tucker!" Stuey was waving his hand and bouncing up and down in his seat.

Hank looked at Stuey coldly.

"What is it, Stuey?" asked Miss Tucker.

"They say you can charm a snake with music. I could bring my violin!"

"I don't think that will be necessary, Stuey," Miss Tucker replied quickly.

Everybody had ideas about finding Puffy.

"I heard that snakes can roll like a hoop," said Jenny Brooks. "They put their tails in their mouths and they roll. So I think we should look out for hoops."

Miss Tucker shook her head. "People believe many things like that about snakes that aren't true, Jenny. You won't find Puffy rolling around like a hoop."

Jenny sat down, very much disappointed.

Hank couldn't help feeling better. Of course he was worried about Puffy. But it was exciting to be the leader of the searching parties.

Hank, Marty, and Buddy were the first ones to go looking for Puffy.

The snake hunters were supposed to look around in the gym first. That was because the gym was right near the Science Room.

As soon as they entered the gym, the boys heard a loud *Hssssssssss!* Hank's heart skipped a beat.

The hissing came from the other side of the room. Right under the window.

The boys tiptoed forward.

Suddenly, a loud *Hssssssssss* made them jump back. But it wasn't Puffy. It was only the radiator.

There was one other moment of hope that morning. That was when Jenny went on an errand for Miss Tucker.

A few minutes later she came running back to the room. "Puffy! I saw Puffy!"

"Where? Where?" Everyone wanted to know.

"Under the closet door in the hall!" Jenny panted, her eyes as big as saucers.

Miss Tucker sent Hank right out with Jenny.

"See! See there! Sticking right out under that closet door!" Jenny drew back a little.

Hank tiptoed over.

It was just a jump rope. Part of a jump rope sticking out of the closet.

Three groups of snake hunters went out that morning. But when the lunch bell rang, there was still no sign of Puffy.

"Hi, Hank," Liz greeted him at lunch. "Everybody's talking about the Great Snake Mystery."

Hank waited. If Liz started teasing him about Puffy, boy, would she be sorry!

"And you don't have to look for him in the auditorium," Liz went on between mouthfuls. "Janey and I looked there this morning."

"Janey!" Hank could hardly believe it.

"Uh-huh! While we were getting the song books out for our class. Janey said she wouldn't touch him. But she helped me look."

Hank sighed. "I wonder if I'll ever see Puffy again."

"Hank," said his mother wearily, "don't you ever think of anything except that snake? Go up and say hello to Benjy. He's lonesome. I do wish I knew what was wrong with him."

Benjy sat up in bed when Hank came in. "Did you find Puffy?" he asked eagerly.

Hank shook his head. "No. He sure made a getaway."

Benjy's eyes filled with tears.

"Aw, we have searching parties out," Hank told him. "We'll find him soon."

How do you like that, Hank thought to himself. Here I am cheering *him* up! Aloud he said, "Sure, Benjy, I bet we find Puffy this afternoon!"

But they didn't.

The searching parties searched and the snake hunters hunted. But no one caught even a glimpse of Puffy.

At three o'clock Miss Tucker asked Hank to stay for a few minutes. She looked rather tired.

"Hank," she said, "Mrs. West has to be told about Puffy the first thing in the morning." Hank was silent.

Miss Tucker put her hand on his shoulder. "You've done a good job taking care of Puffy, Hank. I'm sure he didn't get away because you were careless."

"Then Miss Hill did see me lock the cage, didn't she?"

Miss Tucker smiled. "I didn't even ask Miss Hill. You told me yourself that you were sure you locked it."

Hank stood up a little straighter.

"Well, what do you think, Hank? Can you talk to Mrs. West yourself? Or do you want me to go with you?"

Hank smiled back at Miss Tucker.

She didn't go and ask Miss Hill, he thought proudly.

"It's okay, Miss Tucker," he said. "I'll tell her myself."

The Mystery Is Solved

RIGHT OUTSIDE Mrs. West's office there was a small waiting room. Hank stopped. The door to the waiting room was open. Timidly, he walked in.

Mrs. West was in her office. She was standing by her desk, talking into the telephone. Her back was to the door.

Hank stood waiting nervously. Mrs. West did not turn around. "Yes, yes," she was saying into the phone, "I just got in a few minutes ago. Yes, I just heard about it this morning."

Hank shifted uneasily from one foot to the other.

At last Mrs. West hung up. Before she could turn around, the phone rang again. "Yes, this is Mrs. West," she said. "Oh, no, Mrs. Baker. The snake is quite harmless. No, just one little snake. Yes, quite harmless!"

Hank listened with dismay. Mrs. Baker! Betsy's mother!

Once more Mrs. West hung up. Once more the phone rang. "Mrs. West speaking." Her voice was rising. "Oh, yes, Mr. Blake. I just heard about it a few minutes ago."

Hank wet his lips. Mr. Blake! He was the superintendent of *all* the schools!

"No, Mr. Blake," said Mrs. West, "not yet. I haven't even had a chance to sit down."

If Mr. Blake is calling about Puffy, thought Hank, she'd better sit right down in that chair. . . .

Hank stared. Then he choked back a cry.

THERE ON THE CHAIR WAS PUFFY.

Right behind Mrs. West! Resting cosily on her chair!

Hank stood perfectly still. He could hear his heart pounding.

If he made a sudden grab for Puffy, he might scare him away.

But if Mrs. West sat down ...!

Mrs. West put down the phone. It rang again. "Yes, this is Mrs. West." She reached for her chair without turning. She started to sit down.

Hank stood frozen to the floor.

"A newspaper? Oh, the *Morning News?*" Mrs.

West stood up quickly. "A photographer? A story? What for?"

Hank took a deep breath. He began tiptoeing to the chair.

"Just a minute, please," said Mrs. West.

Hank stopped as if someone had pulled a brake. Then he realized that Mrs. West hadn't even seen him. She was still talking into the phone. "You understand, it's just a harmless little snake," she was saying.

Hank reached the chair. He picked up Puffy.

Mrs. West was beginning to sound quite excited. "Yes, yes," she kept saying. "Of course! Of course! Yes, right out of our Science Room."

Hank tiptoed backward, a step at a time. Just as he got to the door, Mrs. West sat down.

Hank turned and ran. Down the hall he raced with Puffy.

Right into the Science Room.

He closed the door behind him and stood panting.

"Oh, Puffy," he said breathlessly. "You old runaway!" If there were some way to hug a snake, Puffy would have been given a mighty hug then and there.

Quickly, Hank opened Puffy's cage and put him in.

"Stay there, Puffy Jenkins!" Hank told him happily as he locked the cage.

Then he ran back to the fourth grade room to tell the good news.

Puffy was back in his cage.

The fourth grade had finally calmed down.

Mrs. West had been told that Puffy had been found.

Hank didn't even tell Miss Tucker *exactly* where he had found the runaway. It seemed much wiser just to say, "In a chair."

"In a chair?" Miss Tucker repeated.

"Uh-huh," Hank nodded. "Just kind of . . . resting. In a chair."

Miss Tucker looked at Hank for a moment. She didn't ask any more questions.

But Marty did.

"Come on, Hank," he whispered. "Where did you find Puffy?"

Should he tell or shouldn't he? Then, "Swear you'll never tell!" Hank whispered back.

"I'll never tell a soul," Marty promised.

When Hank told him, Marty laughed so hard that he got red in the face. Then he began to choke and had to leave the room to get a drink.

Now that Puffy was back, would he be allowed to stay in school?

"Miss Tucker, will Puffy get in trouble?" the class wanted to know.

"I hope not," was all she would say.

Stuey protested, "It wouldn't be fair to expel him."

"Not fair?" asked Miss Tucker.

"Not without a second chance. Nobody should be expelled from school without a second chance!"

Everyone in the fourth grade agreed.

"Hank," said Miss Tucker at the end of the day, "Mrs. West wants to see us in her office, right away."

Hank gulped, got up, and went along with Miss Tucker.

He didn't know quite what he expected.

But the one thing he didn't expect was to

see Mrs. West smiling happily.

She was sitting at her desk, in THAT CHAIR.

"Come in," said Mrs. West pleasantly. "Come in and sit down."

Hank sat on the edge of his chair.

"I have some excellent news," said Mrs. West. "I think you will be just as pleased as I am."

Miss Tucker and Hank sat in baffled silence.

"Mr. Reynolds called me this morning. He's the editor of the *Morning News,* you know." Mrs. West's smile got broader and broader. "He heard about our snake. He thinks it's just splendid that we have a Science Room with a real snake right in the school. He wants to send a photographer to take pictures and a reporter to write a story about it."

A reporter! A photographer!

Hank was speechless.

"When they do come, Miss Tucker," the principal continued, "I'd like you to explain our Science Room to them. Perhaps it would be a good idea to let Hank answer any questions about the snake. Don't you agree?"

"Of course," murmured Miss Tucker. "Of course."

Hank grinned. Puffy wasn't going to be expelled! And what do you know! He was going to have his picture in the paper!

Hank felt so good he could have done handsprings all the way home.

He raced into the house.

"Hey, Mom! Hey, Liz! I found Puffy! Puffy's back!"

"Well, that's a relief," said Mrs. Jenkins.

"And guess what! Puffy's going to have his picture in the paper!"

"No kidding?" said Liz.

Hank told them what Mrs. West had said about the *Morning News*.

"Maybe they'll take a picture of all of us." Liz looked hopeful. "After all, Puffy's in the family. I'll wear my new red skirt."

Hank looked disgusted. "Don't be dopey! They want a story about a snake, not a skirt!"

He ran upstairs two steps at a time.

"Hey, Benjy, guess what! I found Puffy. He's back!"

To Hank's astonishment, Benjy put his head in his arms and began to cry.

"What's the matter, Benjy? Aren't you glad?"

"I didn't mean to do it, Hank."

"What are you talking about, Benjy?" Hank asked, bewildered.

"I didn't mean to leave the cage open," Benjy sobbed. "I didn't mean to let Puffy out. . . ."

Hank stared at his little brother.

Benjy! Benjy had unlocked the cage. Why hadn't he thought of it before?

"How did it happen?" Hank patted his brother's shoulder. "Tell me, Benjy."

Benjy could hardly talk between sobs.

"That — that day in the Science Room . . . when you told us about Puffy . . . and you didn't even say hello or anything. . . ."

"Yes, yes."

"I just . . . wanted to say hello to Puffy . . . that's all . . . I just opened the cage to say hello to Puffy. . . ."

Of course, thought Hank. The first grade had stayed on in the Science Room. Benjy had opened the cage, but hadn't quite locked it.

And all this time Benjy had been scared. Too scared to go to school. The poor kid!

"Hey, Benjy, quit crying." Hank patted his shoulder again. "It's all right now."

Benjy looked up, his face wet. "What will they do to me?"

"Nothing, Benjy. It's all over. Why, we don't even have to tell anybody how it happened."

For the first time in days, Benjy smiled. "Honest, Hank?"

"Sure, Benjy. It can be our secret. Just you and me. Okay?"

"Forever?" Benjy insisted.

"Forever."

Benjy sighed happily. "I was afraid to tell. I was afraid you'd be awful mad. I was afraid I'd get in trouble in school."

Hank stood up. "Do you think you can go to school tomorrow, Benjy?"

Benjy nodded.

"Want to go early with me? Want to help me give Puffy his breakfast?"

Benjy's eyes danced. "Can I wiggle the stick this time?"

Hank laughed. "Okay. Guess I'll have to show you how."

Benjy started bouncing on the bed.

"Hey, Mommy," he yelled. "I'm hungry!"

Hank grinned. What a dopey kid, he thought. Boy, a kid like that sure needs a big brother.

Hank ran downstairs feeling just like that — like Benjy's big brother. It was a good feeling, too.